THE

MW01045955

A Space Voyage
Hitching a Ride Through the Solar System

by John Bergez

Don Johnston Incorporated
Volo, Illinois

Edited by:

Jerry Stemach, MS, CCC-SLP
Speech/Language Pathologist, Director of Content Development, Start-to-Finish Books

Gail Portnuff Venable, MS, CCC-SLP
Speech/Language Pathologist, San Francisco, California

Dorothy Tyack, MA
Learning Disabilities Specialist, San Francisco, California

Consultant:

Ted S. Hasselbring, PhD
William T. Brian Professor of Special Education Technology, University of Kentucky

Copy Editor:

Susan Kedzior

Cover Design/Illustration:

Karyl Shields, Bill Perry

Interior Illustrations/Photos

Bill Perry, NASA, Corbis

Read by:

Nick Sandys

Sound Engineer/Producer

Tom Krol, *TK Audio Studios*

Audio Producer:

Abel Solorio

Published by:

Don Johnston Incorporated
26799 West Commerce Drive
Volo, IL 60073

800.999.4660 USA Canada
800.889.5242 Technical Support
www.donjohnston.com

DON JOHNSTON

International Standard Book Number
ISBN 1-4105-0022-5

4

This book is dedicated to the memory of the brave crew of the space shuttle Columbia, who gave their lives to the cause of exploring space.

February 1, 2003

A Note on Measurements and Numbers

In this book, you will see two kinds of measurements. The first kind are common American measurements, like pounds and miles. The second are the international measurements used by scientists, like kilograms and kilometers. This chart compares the two systems of measurement.

Distance

American
1 Yard — 36 inches

1 Meter — 39.37 inches
International

American
1 Mile — 5,280 feet

1 Kilometer — 3,274 feet (about 3/5 of a mile)
International

Weight

1 pound = 16 ounces
(American)

You will also see very large numbers. The names of some large numbers are different in the British number system than in the American system used in this book.

American Number System	British Number System
1 million	1 million
1 billion	1 milliard
1 trillion	1 billion

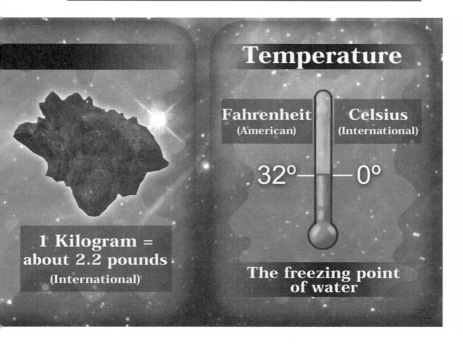

1 Kilogram = about 2.2 pounds (International)

Temperature

Fahrenheit (American)   Celsius (International)

32°—   —0°

The freezing point of water

A comet looks like a fuzzy star with a flowing tail.

Chapter One

Messengers from the Gods

No one knew what they were or where they came from. They were like nothing else in the night sky. They were like bright, fuzzy stars with wispy tails that streamed across the sky like long strands of hair. Their flowing tails made them look as if they were streaking through the heavens.

Yet hour after hour, they seemed to hang
motionless over the Earth. When one of
them appeared in the sky, it would stay
for days or weeks, and then slowly fade
away. The ancient Greeks gave them their
name many centuries ago. They called
them comets, a name that means "hairy
stars."

Many stories were told about comets.
Some people said they were the shining
souls of kings or heroes on their way to
heaven. Others were terrified. They said
comets were messengers sent by the gods
to warn of sickness, war, and death.

In the spring of 1066, one of these
mysterious stars appeared just as King
Harold of England was preparing to fight
against the army of William of Normandy.
William of Normandy wanted to be the
next King of England. He and his men,
the Normans, had been at work in France
building boats to carry their army across

the English Channel to England. When King Harold and William saw the comet, they wondered what it meant.

The comet faded from sight, and William's soldiers crossed the channel to England. The Normans crushed the English army at the Battle of Hastings and King Harold was killed. The victorious William became William the Conqueror, the first in a new line of English kings.

Later, William's wife, Queen Matilda, had a long tapestry made that used pictures to tell the story of the Norman invasion. One scene shows the English pointing in terror at the comet as it hangs in the sky above King Harold. According to the Normans, the comet was a sign that a king would die. Harold was doomed.

Was the comet really a sign from God, as the Normans believed? Or was it just an accident that it appeared when it did?

This scene from a Norman tapestry shows the English
pointing in fear at a comet in the sky above King Harold.

About 600 years later, in 1682, a comet once again glowed in the night sky over England. A scientist named Edmund Halley saw the comet, but instead of being fearful, he was curious. People's understanding of the sky had changed a great deal since the days of William the Conqueror. Back in 1066, people believed that Earth was the center of the universe. They thought the heavens were like a huge dome that circled slowly around the Earth. The stars in the roof of the dome were perfect and never changed.

Comets were frightening because they weren't like the distant, unchanging stars. They appeared suddenly and then mysteriously went away. What could they be, except balls of fire sent by an angry god?

But Halley knew that Earth was not the center of the universe. Halley was an astronomer, a scientist who studies the stars and other objects in space.

He knew that Earth and other planets
travel around the Sun in paths called
orbits. Halley didn't know exactly what
comets were, but he thought they were
natural objects that moved in orbits like
the planets. If the orbits were long
enough, the same comet might disappear
for years and then show up again in
Earth's sky as it made another trip around
the Sun.

After studying records of past comets,
Halley decided that the comet of 1682 was
the same comet that people had seen in
1607 and 1531. He said it had a long,
oval-shaped orbit that took it around the
Sun about every 76 years. "Watch and
see," he said. "This comet will be back in
1758."

Unfortunately, Halley knew he would
be dead years before he could be proved

right or wrong. "If I'm right," he wrote, "I hope the world remembers that it was an Englishman who figured this out."

At six o'clock on Christmas night, 1758, a German farmer peered through a telescope and spotted a fuzzy light among the stars. In the next few weeks, the light got bigger and brighter, and it began to show a long, beautiful tail.

Edmund Halley's prediction had come true. His comet was back, right on schedule. It has been known as Halley's Comet ever since.

Edmund Halley

Today, astronomers know that Halley's Comet has been visiting Earth's skies every 76 years or so for thousands of years. It was Halley's Comet that struck terror into the hearts of the English back in 1066.

More than 1200 years earlier, it had also been seen by Chinese astronomers, who called it a "broom star."

Halley's Comet last swung by the Sun in 1986. Since then, it has been traveling out into space toward the far end of its orbit. There it will turn around and head toward the Sun once again. It will be back in Earth's skies in 2061.

Imagine that you could hitch a ride on Halley's Comet as it begins its sunward journey. Starting from deep in space,

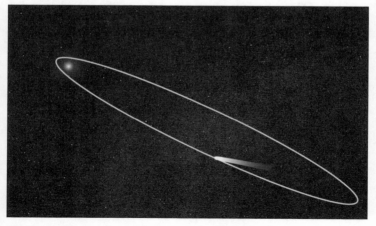

Halley's Comet has a long, oval-shaped orbit.

billions of miles from Earth, you would get a grand tour of our Solar System — the Sun, its planets, and the other objects that move with the Sun through space. And you would get an eye-popping look at what happens to a comet as it emerges from its long winter far in space into a sizzling summer near the blazing Sun. Riding the comet would be the trip of a lifetime — even if it would take half a lifetime to complete!

With the help of your imagination, this book takes you on that voyage through space. But before you set out, it would be good to know what comets are and how they came to be.

The answers lie deep in the past, when our Sun was just an infant star first starting to shine. As you will discover, comets really are messengers after all, with ancient secrets to tell about our own beginnings in the vast, cold space between the stars.

Chapter Two

The Kingdom of the Sun

This chapter tells the story of how comets and the rest of our Solar System came to be. The story is a theory, which means that scientists may change it as they learn new facts. But for now, it is the best explanation we have of how our part of the universe began.

About 5 billion years ago, a cold, dark cloud filled the space where the Solar System is now. This was the cloud that gave birth to the Sun and its planets — and comets, too. It was the parent cloud of our Solar System.

Like everything else in the universe, the matter, or stuff, in that enormous cloud was made of atoms. Atoms are the basic building blocks of matter. They are very, very small — your fingertip has trillions of them!

The early universe was mostly made up of the simplest and smallest atoms, hydrogen and helium. Bigger and more complicated atoms, like those of oxygen or iron, had to be cooked inside stars over millions of years.

Stars act like huge furnaces that forge simple atoms into more complex ones.

At the end of their lives, some giant stars explode. These explosions spray their atoms far out into space, where they can become part of new star systems.

The parent cloud of our Solar System was partly made up of complex atoms from an exploded star. It's a good thing it was, too, because otherwise you would never exist to read this book. The oxygen and iron in our blood, and much of the rest of us as well, are made of atoms that were forged inside a star.

As one scientist has said, "Stars have died so that we might live." You are made of star stuff.

The atoms in the parent cloud took the form of dust and gases. Gases are light, shapeless forms of matter, like the oxygen and nitrogen in the air you breathe. Over millions of years, the gases at the center of the cloud were pulled together by gravity into a gigantic ball, or sphere. Gravity is the force that pulls bits of matter toward each other. For example, Earth's gravity pulls on the gases in our air, keeping them from leaking away into space.

As the gas ball in the center of the cloud became more dense, the ball heated up. Eventually it became so hot that it burst into light, and a star was born — our Sun.

The rest of the parent cloud formed a disk that whirled around the infant Sun. As the disk spun, bits of dust smashed into each other and stuck together, gradually building up into rocky spheres, each with its own gravity. As the spheres grew larger, their gravity attracted still more matter to them.

In this way, four rocky planets were formed. One day, people would call these planets Mercury, Venus, Earth, and Mars.

Farther from the Sun, gravity molded cooler parts of the cloud into four huge spheres.

New planets formed out of the swirling disk of matter that whirled around the infant Sun.

Unlike the inner planets, which were rocky, these outer planets are mostly made of gas. They are called the gas giants: Jupiter, Saturn, Uranus, and Neptune. Still farther out there is a ninth planet, Pluto, a tiny, lonely lump of rock and ice.

Of all the objects that were formed from the parent cloud, the Sun has by far the most matter. The more matter an object has, the stronger its gravity is.

The Sun's powerful gravity makes it the king of the Solar System. All the other objects in the system travel around the Sun, and they are held in their orbits by the pull of the Sun's gravity.

The Sun's gravity reaches across billions of miles of space. To get a picture of how vast the Sun's kingdom is, imagine making a scale model of it. Suppose you put a large yellow beach ball at one end of a soccer field to stand for the Sun.

The planets in the Solar System

Now walk 68 yards (62 meters), about two-thirds of the way to the far end of the field, and put down a pea. The pea stands for Earth.

To show the rest of the Solar System, you'd need more soccer fields. Jupiter would be the size of a tennis ball about three and a half soccer fields from the Sun. To stretch your model all the way to Pluto, you would need 27 soccer fields laid end to end!

Maps of the Solar System often end with Pluto, but the Sun's kingdom extends much farther still. Long ago, beyond the planets, lumps of dust and ice from the parent cloud settled into their own orbits. And there most of them stayed, billions upon billions of dirty icebergs drifting peacefully in the deep freeze of outer space.

A comet is a dirty iceberg.

Far from the Sun's heat, these icebergs have not changed at all in nearly 5 billion years. They are perfectly preserved bits of the cloud that created our Solar System — and, eventually, created you and me.

We can't yet go out and fetch one of these icebergs to study, billions of miles from Earth. Luckily, though, sometimes the icebergs come to us.

They come as comets.

For that is what comets are — big, dirty icebergs or snowballs more ancient than Earth. Every now and then, something — perhaps the gravity of a passing star — gives one of these icebergs a push and sends it on a long, slow fall toward the Sun. During the comet's fall, the gravity of the Sun and planets changes its orbit. Some comets end up in orbits so large that they take thousands of years to make one trip around the Sun.

Some get flung out of the Solar System altogether.

And some, like Halley's Comet, settle into smaller orbits that bring them to Earth's skies again and again.

Comets that come near enough for astronomers to study are priceless treasures. They are messengers from a time before Earth was born.

So how does a dirty iceberg turn into a glowing ball with a long, shining tail? You'll find out as you ride Halley's Comet to the Sun.

But first you must travel deep into space and catch up to Halley's at the far end of its orbit, beyond the planet Neptune. Look, you can see it now, a mountainous shadow tumbling slowly through the darkness of space. The year is 2024, and Halley's is just about to turn and head back for another trip around our home star, the Sun.

And now, climb aboard. It's time to hitch a ride on a comet.

Chapter Three

2024: Pluto

You've arrived on Halley's Comet, drifting through space between the orbits of Neptune and Pluto, more than 3 billion miles (about 4¹/₂ billion kilometers) from the Sun. At this distance, the Sun looks like a bright star. Out here, it is always night, and colder than you can imagine. Without a space suit, you would instantly freeze to death. (You did remember to bring a space suit, didn't you?)

You are standing on a potato-shaped iceberg, about 10 miles (16 kilometers) long and 5 miles (8 kilometers) wide. If you set up some searchlights, you can make out hills, valleys, and even a small mountain or two.

You might be surprised to see that Halley's looks more like a gigantic lump of coal than an iceberg. That's because its surface is coated with a crust of black dust. If you dig down below the crust, you'll find that Halley's Comet is made of ice mixed with dust.

The iceberg carries you along in an eerie silence. You've probably seen movies where spacecraft whoosh through space and blow each other up in thunderous explosions. Well, that only happens in the movies. The truth is that there is no air in space to carry sound, so Halley's glides through the night as silently as a ghost.

A view from Halley's Comet

In space, you can set off the biggest explosion you want, and it wouldn't make the slightest sound.

There would be sound on Halley's if it had an atmosphere, or layer of air. But Halley's gravity is too weak to hold an atmosphere. Of course, that also means there is no air to breathe — another reason why you need that space suit.

All around you the sky is inky-black and filled with stars — many more stars than you have ever seen on the clearest night on Earth. But the stars don't twinkle as they do back home. It's Earth's atmosphere that makes the stars sparkle. On Halley's, the stars shine steadily and in many colors, like thousands upon thousands of Christmas lights — blue and red and orange and yellow as well as white.

Stars are different colors because they burn at different temperatures. Cooler stars are red or orange.

Yellow stars like our Sun are hotter.
White stars are hotter still. The hottest
stars are a dazzling blue. Our Sun is
medium-hot — for a star.

One of the countless points of light in
the sky isn't a star at all, but the planet
Pluto, orbiting the Sun even farther out
than Halley's. Like the other planets,
Pluto shines because it reflects the Sun's
light. Why don't you take out a telescope
and have a look at it?

When you look at Pluto close-up, you
might think you're seeing double. Pluto
has a moon, Charon, which is almost half
as big as Pluto itself. Bound by gravity,
Pluto and Charon circle each other in a
slow dance as they travel together around
the Sun. Many astronomers call Pluto a
double planet.

Other astronomers say that Pluto isn't
really a planet at all. As planets go, Pluto
is a midget, smaller than Earth's moon. In
fact, it might better be called a large comet!

A view of Pluto from Charon

Like Halley's Comet, Pluto is mostly a lump of ice, although it has a rocky core. It may simply be one of the nearest of those ancient icebergs that travel in long orbits beyond Neptune.

Pluto's orbit is so huge that it takes 248 Earth years for Pluto to make one trip around the Sun. A planet's year is the time it takes the planet to make one round-trip in its orbit. An Earth year is 365 days, but a Pluto year is 248 times as long. If you had been born on Pluto, you'd have a very long wait between birthdays.

Besides being long, Pluto's orbit is tilted compared to the orbits of the other planets, as you can see in the picture on the next page. Pluto's strange orbit sometimes takes it inside the orbit of Neptune. So when we say Pluto is the farthest planet from the Sun, we're only right most of the time. Sometimes Neptune is the farthest planet.

Pluto's orbit is tilted compared to the orbits of the other planets, like Neptune.

Pluto was named for the ancient Greek god of the underworld, the cold, dark place where souls went when people died. Charon was named for the boatman who took the souls across the River Styx to the underworld. The names fit, because on Pluto and Charon, it is always freezing night.

On Earth, we humans think it's cold when the temperature drops much below 32 degrees on the Fahrenheit scale or zero degrees on the Celsius scale. This is the temperature where water freezes into ice. When scientists measure temperature, they usually use the Celsius scale.

On Pluto, you'd be lucky if the temperature got as high as 350 degrees below zero Fahrenheit (about 200 degrees below zero Celsius). When Pluto is farthest from the Sun, its thin atmosphere freezes and coats the planet's surface with ice.

A view of the Sun from Pluto

You wouldn't miss Pluto's atmosphere anyway. Besides being too thin to breathe, it is made of gases that would be poisonous to humans.

While you've been looking at Pluto, something has been happening to your iceberg. You can't feel it, but the Sun's gravity is tugging on Halley's. Slowly at first, and then faster and faster as time goes on, you are being pulled toward the Sun.

The closer an object is to the Sun, the harder the Sun's gravity tugs on it, and the faster it goes. All during your trip Halley's will be picking up speed, like a roller coaster going downhill.

Already, you're racing through the night faster than the fastest jet. But even at this speed, it takes an awfully long time to get anywhere. The planets are so far apart that it will take about 18 years just to get to the orbit of the next planet, Neptune.

I hope you brought along some good books to read.

Chapter Four

Neptune and Uranus

For nearly 20 years, Halley's speeds silently through the darkness of space. You might think you would see the stars go whizzing by you, but they never seem to move. The stars are so far away that they look the same even though you are traveling across millions of miles.

When you look at the stars, you are seeing places far beyond the farthest limits of the Solar System. As big as the Sun's kingdom is, it is only a tiny island in the vast ocean of space.

Finally, you approach the orbit of Neptune. You are entering the land of the gas giants, the huge planets that could swallow up dozens of Earths.

Neptune was named for the ancient Roman god of the sea. In your telescope, Neptune is a beautiful, greenish-blue sphere. What you are seeing is really the top of its thick clouds. The clouds are made of gases — mostly hydrogen and helium, plus a little methane, the gas that on Earth we call marsh gas. The tops of the clouds are icy cold — nearly as cold as Pluto.

Actually, Neptune's clouds make up most of the planet. Like the other giant planets, Neptune has no solid surface to stand on. It is mostly a great balloon of gas.

Deep in the atmosphere, this gas changes to liquid and then becomes slushy ice surrounding a rocky core.

Neptune is the smallest of the four gas giants, but it is still huge. Its sphere has as much room inside it as 50 planets the size of Earth!

From a distance Neptune looks peaceful, but those beautiful blue clouds are whipping around the planet at furious speeds. Neptune's howling winds reach more than 1200 miles (2000 kilometers) per hour. Neptune wouldn't be your best choice for kite flying, even if you could stand the cold.

If you look closely in the space around Neptune, you can see six thin rings circling the planet. All the giant planets have rings around them, but until the late twentieth century, humans only knew about the bright rings around the planet Saturn. The rings around the other gas giants are so dark that it took powerful telescopes and close-up pictures from spacecraft to reveal them.

As you look at Neptune, you also spot at least eight moons orbiting the planet. The largest of these moons is called Triton. In ancient Greek mythology, Triton was a son of Neptune, the god of the sea.

Triton is a fascinating and colorful place. It is coated with pink and bluish ice made of frozen nitrogen and methane. In liquid form, nitrogen can get extremely cold without freezing. Sometimes spectacular volcanoes erupt on Triton, spraying liquid nitrogen nearly 30,000 feet (over 9,000 meters) into the sky.

Triton is the coldest place in the Solar System. Those pretty pink and blue ices are about 400 degrees below zero Fahrenheit (235 degrees below zero Celsius).

Neptune and Triton might be interesting places to see, but I doubt that you'd want to live there. Do you suppose the next planet will be any friendlier?

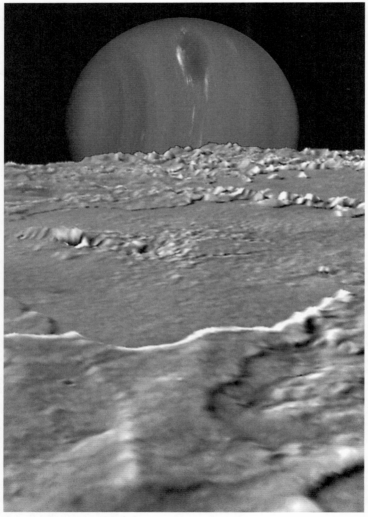

A view of Neptune from Triton   *NASA*

To find out, you have to wait another 11 years while Halley's crosses the empty miles to the orbit of Uranus.

By the time you get there, you've been traveling on Halley's for nearly 30 years. Babies who were born back on Earth when your journey began are fathers and mothers by now. But you've still only reached the seventh planet from the Sun.

Uranus was named after the ancient Greek god of the heavens, the grandfather of the mighty god Zeus. Uranus is almost a twin of Neptune, a huge, cold ball of greenish-blue clouds driven by powerful winds.

Compared to the other planets, Uranus is a topsy-turvy world. All the planets, and the Sun as well, rotate around an axis, like spinning tops. The axis is an imaginary line that extends through an object's north and south poles. Earth, for example, makes one complete turn around its axis every 24 hours.

This rotation gives us day and night as our side of the planet points toward, or away from, the Sun. But Uranus is tipped over on its side, so that its axis points sideways, as you can see in the picture on this page. Astronomers think that some huge object, perhaps as large as Earth,

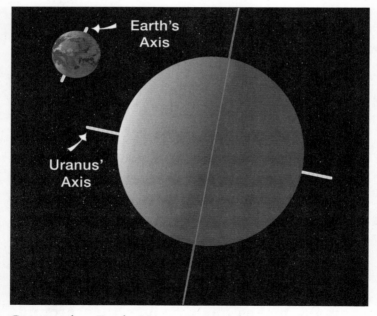

Compared to Earth, Uranus is tipped on its side. The axis of Uranus points sideways, so that sometimes its north or south pole points at the Sun.

smashed into Uranus long ago and knocked it on its side.

The result is that Uranus has some very strange seasons. Uranus takes 84 Earth years to make one trip around the Sun. For one fourth of its orbit, its north pole points at the Sun and enjoys a summer that lasts for 21 Earth years. During all this time, the Sun never sets on the northern half of the planet. But the Sun is so far away that even summer is a long, dim twilight there.

During another 21 years, the south pole points at the Sun, and the planet's northern half is plunged into a cold, lightless winter, never seeing a sunrise. During spring and fall, the Sun rises and sets each day a little farther north or south, so that it appears to move gradually from one pole to the other.

Uranus has 11 coal-black rings that circle its equator, the halfway point between the north and south poles. Because Uranus is tipped on its side, its rings make it look like a gigantic bull's-eye.

Besides the rings, Uranus has at least 21 moons sprinkled around it. The view from one of these moons would be something to

Uranus

see, with Uranus hanging in the night sky like a big blue-green balloon, surrounded by its black rings and its family of little worlds.

But for breathtaking sights, nothing compares with the next planet you are about to see.

Saturn

Chapter Five

Saturn

You glide through space for six more years before you reach the orbit of the next planet, Saturn. The Sun is slowly growing brighter as you get closer, so that noon on Halley's is getting about as bright as twilight on Earth. In the dim light, you can go exploring, taking huge leaps as you go. In Halley's weak gravity, you can jump high into the sky and take hours to float gently down to the surface!

Like the planets, Halley's rotates, but very slowly. It takes a little more than 7 Earth days to make one complete turn on its axis. So daylight lasts about half an Earth week, plenty of time for looking around and doing slow cartwheels in space. When the Sun finally sets, you have half a week of darkness to sleep!

By the time you get to the orbit of Saturn, you're probably impatient to see something new. But the wait turns out to be worth it.

Even through small telescopes on Earth, Saturn is a thrilling sight. From Halley's, you get a view that takes your breath away: a huge, pale yellow ball surrounded by dazzling rings.

Each of Saturn's rings looks like a solid band at first. But when you look closely, you see stars shining through the rings, so you know they can't be solid.

Saturn's rings are actually billions of bits of ice that circle the planet like tiny moons, sparkling as they catch the sunlight. The brightest rings spread out over more than 45,000 miles (74,000 kilometers). But they are very thin, less than a mile deep.

If you could dive into Saturn's rings, you would find yourself surrounded by glittering chunks of ice. Some chunks are too small to see without a microscope, but others are the size of snowflakes, hailstones, and snowballs. Some are as big as boulders. A few are mountain-sized icebergs. You could swim around inside the rings by pushing off against one chunk of ice and floating through space to another.

How did Saturn get its glorious rings? Astronomers aren't sure. Possibly, an icy moon wandered too close to Saturn, and the planet's powerful gravity broke the moon into tiny pieces. Or a comet like Halley's may have smashed into a moon, spraying icy bits of the comet and the moon into space, where they collected into rings.

You could swim inside Saturn's rings by pushing off one
chunk of ice and floating to another.

Wherever they came from, Saturn's rings make it the jewel of the Solar System. There is nothing else like it in all the Sun's kingdom.

Saturn itself is huge, big enough to hold more than 700 Earths inside it. But compared to Earth, Saturn is a ball of fluff. Like the other giant planets, it is mostly made of gas and liquid. The most amazing thing about Saturn is how lightly this matter is packed together.

Different kinds of matter are packed more or less closely together. This is called density. For example, wood has a lower density than water, which is why wood floats.

Saturn has the lowest density of all the planets. In fact, like wood, Saturn is less dense than water. If you had a bathtub big enough, Saturn would float in it like a gigantic beach ball! (Astronomers like to joke that it would leave a ring.)

Like the other gas giants, Saturn has powerful winds in its atmosphere. Around the planet's middle, or equator, the winds blow at 1100 miles (nearly 1800 kilometers) per hour. Sometimes great storms bubble up to the top of Saturn's clouds, where they can be seen in telescopes on Earth.

The tops of Saturn's clouds are extremely cold, as you would expect at this distance from the Sun. Deep inside, though, Saturn is blazing hot. Something is going on in its core that causes Saturn to give out more heat than it gets from the Sun.

Saturn's rings make it an unforgettable sight, but the moons around the planet are wonderful, too. So far, astronomers have counted 30 of them!

The biggest of Saturn's moons, Titan, is a planet-sized world, a little bigger than the planet Mercury. Titan is the only moon in the Solar System that has a thick atmosphere. When you look at Titan through your telescope, all you can see is an orange-brown smog. Like Earth's air, this atmosphere is mostly made up of nitrogen.

Scientists are eager to find out what Titan's surface is like under the smog, because Titan may hold clues to how life began on Earth. In important ways, the conditions on Titan may be like those on Earth billions of years ago.

Scientists should know a lot more about Saturn and Titan by the time of your ride on Halley's. In 1997, a spacecraft was launched from Earth that was due to reach Saturn in 2004. If all went well, the spacecraft sent a package of scientific instruments to Titan's surface.

A view of Saturn from Titan

The planet Saturn was named after a Roman god who was the father of Jupiter. Jupiter rebelled against Saturn and became the greatest of the gods. And, as you will soon see, the planet Jupiter is truly the lord of the planets.

Chapter Six

Jupiter

As you pass Saturn's orbit, Halley's continues to pick up speed. Remember, the closer you get to the Sun, the faster you go. By Earth standards, you're really moving now — about 24,000 miles (nearly 39,000 kilometers) per hour. At this rate, you should reach the next planet, Jupiter, in no time.

Well, it takes another two years, but here you are.

You've already seen three giant planets, but mighty Jupiter is the biggest of all. *All* the other planets of the Solar System would fit inside Jupiter, with room to spare!

Jupiter's huge size means that it has a lot of matter in it, and so its gravity is very strong. For this reason, Jupiter isn't the place to go if you want to lose weight. The harder that gravity pulls on you, the more you weigh. If you weigh 100 pounds (220 kilograms) on Earth, you would weigh 254 pounds (600 kilograms) on Jupiter! (On Halley's, you don't weigh much more than a string bean.)

Luckily for you, Halley's doesn't pass too close to the lord of the planets. If it did, Jupiter's tremendous gravity could change Halley's orbit and send you on a one-way trip out of the Solar System. Even worse, Jupiter's gravity could suck your iceberg right into the planet itself.

In July 1994, people on Earth got to see what happens when a comet smashes into Jupiter. The unlucky comet was called Shoemaker-Levy, after the people who discovered it.

As it got close to Jupiter, the comet broke up into chunks. The chunks were pulled in by Jupiter's gravity and slammed into the atmosphere with the force of millions of atom bombs, burning up in huge fireballs. These gigantic explosions left dark scars in Jupiter's clouds that could be seen even through small telescopes on Earth.

Imagine that you could parachute gently into Jupiter's atmosphere instead of smashing into it. You would find yourself traveling down through icy-cold clouds of hydrogen. Furious winds swirl through the clouds at hundreds of miles per hour, creating huge storms complete with flashing lightning.

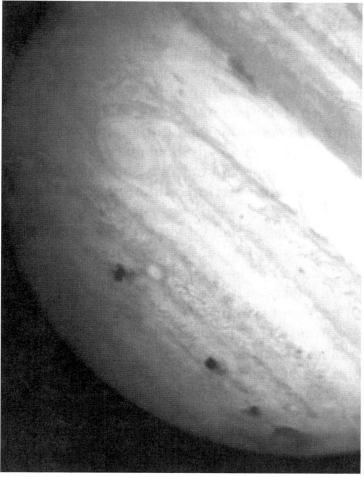

The black spots on Jupiter in this picture are the scars left when pieces of Comet Shoemaker-Levy smashed into the planet. The biggest scar, in the lower right part of the picture, is the size of Earth. *NASA*

Falling deeper into the clouds, you would soon be lost in total darkness. The deeper you go, the more Jupiter's gravity squeezes the atmosphere, making it more and more dense. The atmosphere's gases gradually turn into liquid, and then into a kind of melted metal around Jupiter's rocky core. Like Saturn, Jupiter is extremely hot toward the center — five times hotter than the surface of the Sun!

But don't bother worrying about being roasted. If you've ever gone diving in the ocean, you know that the deeper you go, the more pressure you feel. On Jupiter, the pressure of the atmosphere would crush you even if you could stand the heat.

One way or the other, exploring Jupiter would mean certain death. So it's just as well that you're watching from a safe distance on Halley's.

From out here, Jupiter is beautiful to look at, with colorful bands that are actually great belts of winds. Among the bands are oval patterns where the winds swirl into hurricanes. One of these storm systems is known as the Great Red Spot.

This one vast storm could swallow up two planets the size of Earth. The storm has lasted for hundreds of years.

A close-up view of some of the swirling clouds in Jupiter's atmosphere. The large oval is the Great Red Spot.

As you watch the Great Red Spot, you might notice that Jupiter is spinning very fast. You can see the Great Red Spot disappear around one side of Jupiter and then come back around the other side several hours later. As huge as Jupiter is, it spins completely around every 10 hours!

You also see rings around Jupiter that are made of dark reddish dust. In your telescope, they look like thin smoke rings.

Like Saturn, Jupiter has many moons — at least 39 of them. One moon, Io, is the most violent world in the Solar System. Jupiter's gravity squeezes Io, melting its insides and causing volcanoes that blast hot gases and ash nearly 200 miles (300 kilometers) into the sky. The gases contain a lot of sulfur, making Io stink like rotten eggs.

Io's constant volcanoes have left scars on its surface and turned it red. One scientist has said, "I've seen better-looking pizzas."

Another of Jupiter's moons, icy Europa, may be one of the best places in the Solar System to look for life beyond Earth.

Io

All the forms of life that we know about need water, and scientists believe that Europa's thick crust of ice floats on a salty ocean of water.

On Earth, most living things get their energy from the Sun. But there are tiny forms of life called bacteria at the bottom of Earth's oceans that don't need sunlight. Scientists have also found bacteria living inside the ice near the North and South Poles. These discoveries give astronomers hope that life might be found on Europa as well.

As you leave Jupiter and its moons behind, you are less than a year away from sweeping by Earth on your way to the Sun. Back home, people are starting to hear a lot about Halley's Comet now. But where is it? All you've got out here is a lump of dirty ice. If something doesn't happen soon, there isn't going to be much for people to see in 2061!

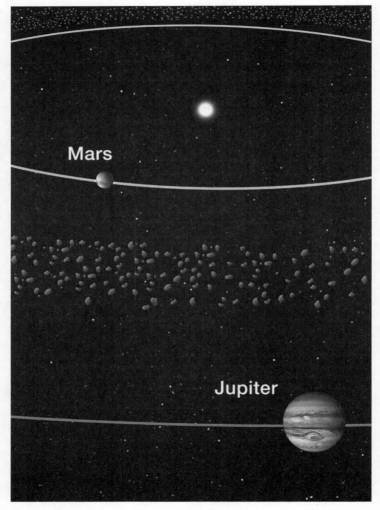

The asteroid belt is a swarm of rocks between Jupiter and Mars.

Chapter Seven

The
Asteroid Belt

After leaving Jupiter, you fly by a vast region of space known as the asteroid belt. The asteroid belt is a swarm of rocks that orbit the Sun. They are like pieces of a planet that never got put together.

In fact, that is probably just what the asteroid belt is — a would-be planet that somehow failed to come together in the parent cloud that created the Solar System. Instead, chunks of rock and metal were left to litter the space between Jupiter and Mars, each traveling in its own orbit.

The picture at the beginning of this chapter shows the asteroid belt on a map of the Solar System. But don't be fooled into thinking that asteroids are crowded close together. They only look that way from a great distance. On average, more than a million miles separate one asteroid from another.

Asteroids are tiny worlds. Some are only as big as boulders. The largest are hundreds

A view of an asteroid from a spacecraft   *NASA* of miles wide — still very small, compared to planets.

But even small asteroids become huge bombs when they strike a planet or a moon at extremely high speeds. This can happen when Jupiter's gravity changes an asteroid's orbit and sets it up to collide with another world.

Earth has been hit many times by both asteroids and comets. Many scientists believe that a number of such collisions helped to kill off the dinosaurs 65 million years ago. The impacts of these collisions caused huge tidal waves, started forest fires, and kicked up enough dust to darken the skies all over Earth for a year or more.

Could such a terrifying event happen again? A major collision is nearly certain to happen someday. Scientists are now looking for ways to intercept an incoming asteroid or comet and change its path so it won't collide with Earth.

As you pass the asteroid belt, you are crossing the boundary between the inner and outer Solar System. Behind you are the gas giants. Up ahead, nearer the Sun, are the smaller, rocky planets.

It is just about here, nearly 37 years after Halley's began its long fall toward the Sun, that something starts to happen to your iceberg.

Have you heard the story of the ugly duckling who grew up to be a beautiful swan? Up to now, Halley's has been like the ugly duckling — a cold, dark lump that doesn't shine with the beauty of the stars or the planets. But that is starting to change.

Although it's still unbearably cold for you on the comet, Halley's is getting close enough to the Sun to feel its heat. You hardly notice at first, but bits of the iceberg's frozen surface are starting to steam. Tiny specks of dust are freed from the ice, and they float around you, shining like fireflies as they catch the sunlight.

As Halley's dust floats away, some of the ice beneath starts to turn to gas in the Sun's heat and goes streaming away into space. Before long, you are surrounded by a fine mist of gas and dust. A white haze starts to fill your sky, though you can still see the stars shining through it.

As Halley's warms up, ice near the surface turns to gas, sending a white mist streaming into the sky.

The mist shines in the sunlight and grows and grows until it forms a huge sphere around the iceberg more than 100,000 miles (160,000 kilometers) wide — more than 10 times as big as the Earth!

This bright, misty cloud is called the coma of the comet. The solid part of Halley's is in the center. It's called the nucleus. When people look at the head of a comet, what they see is the huge, shining coma, not the iceberg inside.

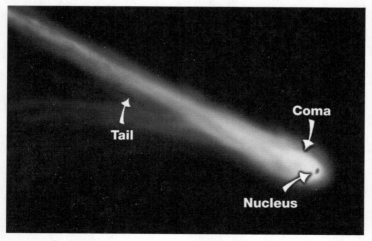

Parts of a comet

As the coma spreads, some of its gases and dust are pushed away from the Sun by the solar wind. The solar wind isn't a movement of air, like the winds on Earth. It is made up of invisible particles that are hurtling away from the Sun at tremendous speeds.

You can't feel the solar wind, but the gases and dust in the coma are so light that the slight pressure of the solar wind drives them backward into a long streak of glowing matter. Suddenly, Halley's has a tail, shining brightly with reflected sunlight.

Have you ever looked at a sunbeam and seen tiny bits of dust swimming in the air? A comet's tail is much thinner than that stream of dust. In fact, it is about as close to nothing as you can get. You could pass right through the tail and never feel it. It would be like walking through a sunbeam.

The heat of the Sun turns a dirty iceberg into a beautiful comet with a shining coma and tail.

Like the coma, Halley's tail grows and grows until it stretches behind you for millions of miles. When people on Earth look up at Halley's now, they will see a glowing ball with a long, milky-white tail — one of the most beautiful sights in Earth's skies.

At long last, your ugly duckling has become a swan.

Chapter Eight

Mars

By the time you reach the orbit of Mars, your comet is a glorious sight. It's a shame there's no one on Mars to watch you go by.

In the past, people believed there *were* creatures on Mars — creatures who might invade the Earth. On Halloween night in 1938, thousands of frightened Americans fled their homes when they heard a radio broadcast of a science fiction story called *The War of the Worlds*. A breathless announcer said that octopus-like Martians had landed in New Jersey and were killing humans with death rays. People who tuned in late thought the invasion was really happening!

As it turned out, Earth invaded Mars first. Since the 1970s, a number of unmanned spacecraft have landed on Mars and tested the soil for signs of life. So far, they haven't found any Martians, not even a Martian germ.

Instead, they found a cold, dry desert of red dust, sand, and rock. Mars was named after the Roman god of war because the reddish color of the planet reminded people of blood. Mars is often called the Red Planet.

What makes Mars red? The Martian soil is rich in iron that oxygen has turned into rust. You might call Mars the Rusty Planet.

When you look at Mars through your telescope, you can spot two small, rocky moons. They are called Phobos and Deimos, after two Greek gods who were helpers to the god of war. Most likely, they are asteroids that were captured by the gravity of Mars long ago.

Mars is the first planet you've seen on your trip that has a solid surface to explore. Of course, you would need your space suit. For one thing, you couldn't breathe the Martian air. The air on Mars is mostly carbon dioxide, the gas that makes the bubbles in soft drinks.

In this picture of Mars, the small circle of white at the top is the ice cap at one of the Martian poles.

The ice caps at the planet's north and south poles are frozen carbon dioxide, which on Earth we call "dry ice."

The Martian atmosphere is very thin, much thinner than the air at high altitudes on Earth. If you've ever camped in high mountains, you may know that it takes less heat to boil water as the air pressure gets thinner. On Mars, the pressure of the atmosphere is so light that watery liquids turn instantly to steam, or vapor. If you stepped on Mars without a space suit, the heat of your body would make your blood boil and turn to steam.

You'd also need your space suit to keep from freezing to death. On average, Mars is 50 million miles (80 million kilometers) farther from the Sun than Earth, so it can be bitterly cold. But sometimes it's toasty compared to the outer planets. Mars travels in an oval-shaped orbit that brings it closer to the Sun at some times than at others. On a hot summer day, Mars can get as warm as 68 degrees Fahrenheit (20 degrees Celsius).

Warm weather on Mars brings fierce winds that kick up huge dust storms, sometimes covering the entire planet with a choking red haze. But once the dust settled down, you could go roaming over a spectacular landscape of blood-red mountains, deep canyons, and wide craters.

Mars has some amazing features to explore. Its biggest mountain, Olympus Mons, is a volcano that is 16 miles (25 kilometers) high — three times as high as Mount Everest, the tallest mountain on Earth. And one tremendous system of

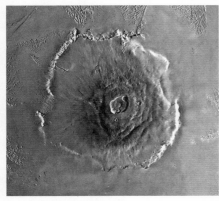

canyons, called Valles Marineris, makes the Grand Canyon in Arizona look like just a little ditch. It's four times deeper than the Grand

Olympus Mons   *NASA*

Canyon and stretches across 2500 miles (4000 kilometers) — the distance from New York to Los Angeles!

Perhaps the most exciting features on Mars are the scars that look like dry riverbeds. These scars in the Martian surface may mean that fresh water gushed there long ago. And where there was water, there may have been life.

Early in its history, Mars was much warmer and wetter than it is today. For a time, it may have had fast-flowing rivers, wide lakes, and possibly even oceans.

All of that water is gone from the surface now. Some of it leaked away into space. Some of it sank deep into the Martian soil, and it may still be there in the form of ice. And some of it is trapped underneath the ice caps at the planet's north and south poles.

Did life start on Mars billions of years ago, before water disappeared from its surface? Many scientists hope so.

Perhaps in our lifetime, Earth will send explorers to Mars.

They think that future explorers might find traces, or fossils, of plants and animals in Martian rocks. Simple forms of life, such as bacteria, may still be living deep under the Martian surface today.

Finding Martian life, or even fossils, would be thrilling. It would be a sign that life can happen anywhere in the universe where the conditions are right.

Perhaps in our lifetime, Earth will send astronauts to take a closer look at Mars. If so, it will be the greatest adventure any human explorer has ever had.

Chapter Nine

Venus and Mercury

A few weeks after leaving Mars behind, you fly past the orbit of Earth. Hundreds of thousands of miles away, people back home are gazing up at you, marveling at the sight of Halley's Comet returning after 75 years.

Of course, they won't see you waving. You are lost in the glow of Halley's huge coma. But you'll get another chance to say hello when Halley's passes Earth again after looping around the Sun.

Up ahead is the planet Venus. Venus, named for the Roman goddess of love and beauty, is one of the loveliest and brightest lights in Earth's skies. You may know it as the Evening Star.

Venus is nearly the same size as Earth. At one time, it was called Earth's sister planet. Because Venus is closer to the Sun than Earth is, some people imagined that Venus was a tropical paradise.

The truth is a little different.

Our "sister planet" turns out to be a roasting-hot world cloaked in foul-smelling, poisonous clouds. High above the surface, the thick clouds are made mostly of sulfuric acid. The rain from these clouds would eat through the roof of a car.

Below the high clouds, the air on Venus is not only deadly to breathe, it is extremely heavy. It weighs down on the surface with the kind of pressure you would feel under nearly a mile of water on Earth. No matter how hard you tried to run on Venus, you would find yourself moving in slow motion, like a diver on the ocean floor.

You wouldn't feel much like running around on Venus anyway. The gases in its dense atmosphere trap the Sun's heat, keeping it from leaking away into space. Scientists call this the *greenhouse effect*. Greenhouses are the buildings on Earth that are used to grow plants that need warm temperatures. But on Venus, the atmosphere creates a "runaway" greenhouse effect, one that is out of control. The clouds trap the planet's heat so well that the temperature on the surface is 880 degrees Fahrenheit (472 degrees Celsius). That's hot enough to melt lead! Even worse, because of the greenhouse effect, Venus never cools down, not even at night.

   As you might expect, Venus is not
only unbearably hot, it is extremely dry.
Venus probably had large amounts of
water at one time, but the water boiled
away long ago.

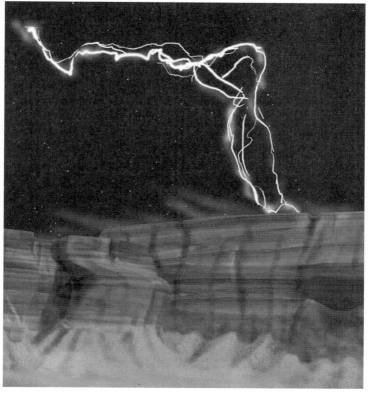

Venus is a broiling-hot, bone-dry desert.

A day on this broiling hot desert of a planet would be unpleasant, to say the least. It would also be very long. Venus rotates very slowly, making one complete turn on its axis every 243 Earth days. That's actually a little longer than a Venus year, the time it takes Venus to go once around the Sun. So, from sunrise to sunrise, a Venus day is actually longer than a Venus year!

All things considered, Venus probably isn't the place to spend your next summer vacation.

As you pass by Venus, you are nearing the sunward end of Halley's long orbit. In between Halley's and the Sun is the planet Mercury.

Mercury was named for the speedy messenger of the Roman gods. The closer an object is to the Sun, the faster it travels in its orbit. As the closest planet to the Sun, Mercury is naturally the fastest. It zips around its orbit in only 88 Earth days. If you lived on Mercury, you could celebrate New Year's every three months! Earth months, that is.

But you probably don't want to live on Mercury any more than you want to spend your summer vacation on Venus. You might guess that Mercury is very hot, since it is so near the Sun. And you'd be right — but only some of the time. Unlike Venus, Mercury doesn't have an atmosphere to keep its heat from escaping into space, so at night, Mercury is deadly *cold* — as much as 279 degrees below zero Fahrenheit (173 degrees below zero Celsius).

At night, Mercury is freezing cold. Its surface looks a lot like Earth's moon, with big craters left by collisions with asteroids and other space rocks.

Mercury heats up fast during the day, but it never gets quite as hot as Venus. Still, by the middle of the morning on Mercury you could roast a chicken without an oven. Unfortunately, you'd be roasted, too.

Like Venus, Mercury rotates very slowly, so its days are very long. Mercury only makes one and a half turns on its axis in the time it takes for it to go once around the Sun (a Mercury year). So a year on Mercury is only a day and a half long in Mercury time! Calendars on Venus and Mercury would be very weird.

You should be glad that Halley's doesn't get as near to the Sun as Mercury does. Comets that pass closer to the Sun often break into pieces in the ferocious heat. Some comets even come in from space on one-way orbits that send them plunging directly into the Sun.

Luckily for you, Halley's path takes it safely around the Sun, keeping it (and you) from dying a fiery death. But as you approach the Sun, Halley's whole surface seems to be erupting in the heat. Patches of ice are bubbling, and the ground is cracking under your feet as more and more of Halley's ice turns to gas. Towering fountains are bursting out all around you, sending vapors streaming into the coma. Soon you are surrounded by a blinding white blizzard of shining gases and dust.

No place on the iceberg's surface is safe anymore. This would be a good time to dig yourself a deep shelter in one of Halley's hills while you ride out the fury of the Sun.

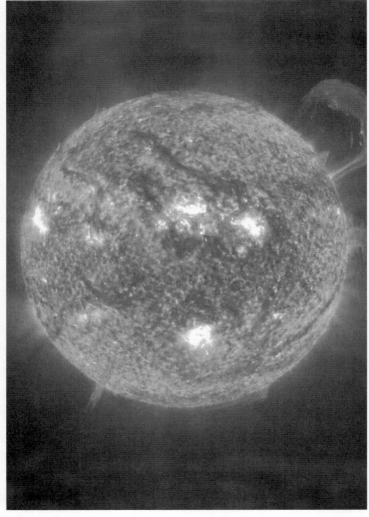

The Sun   *NASA*

Chapter Ten

The Sun

It is July 2061. Halley's is being pulled hard by the Sun's gravity now. It whips around the Sun like a roller coaster screaming around a turn and begins to speed back the way it came.

The Sun is the true giant of the Solar System. More than one million Earths would fit inside this blazing ball of gas!

The Sun, of course is, *very* hot —
nearly 11,000 degrees Fahrenheit (6,000
degrees Celsius) at the surface, and 27
million degrees Fahrenheit (15 million
degrees Celsius) deep inside.

The Sun sheds heat and light as it
forges millions of tons of hydrogen into
helium every second. It gives out more
energy *in one second* than all the people
on Earth have produced in all of history.
Yet this awesome furnace is only one star
among countless billions of stars in the
universe.

The Sun is part of a great system of
stars called the Milky Way Galaxy. Like
the Solar System, our galaxy is held
together by gravity.

From the outside, our galaxy would
look like a pinwheel with spiral arms.
The Sun is located on one of the arms, far
from the galaxy's center.

The galaxy is huge. Astronomers
estimate that it contains 200 billion stars!

The Milky Way Galaxy

Numbers like this are too big to understand easily, so let's try a little thought experiment. Suppose you counted the stars in our galaxy nonstop at a rate of one per second. How long do you think it would take to count them?

A month? Six months? A year?

The answer is 6,341 years. And our galaxy is only one of *billions* of galaxies in the universe.

Obviously, the universe is a very large place, especially when you consider the distances between stars and galaxies. These distances are so huge that astronomers use a special measure called a *light year* to talk about them.

A light year isn't a measure of time. Instead, it's the distance that light travels in one year. Light is the fastest thing in the universe — a beam of light could circle the Earth 7 times in a single second.

In a year, light travels nearly 6 trillion miles (9.5 trillion kilometers).

The nearest star to our Sun is 4.2 light years away, or about 25 trillion miles (40 trillion kilometers). The nearest *galaxy* is the Andromeda Galaxy, 2.2 *million* light years away.

In dark skies, away from city lights, you can spot Andromeda from Earth without a telescope. A book about the night sky can tell you where and when to look. Andromeda will be a fuzzy patch of light among the stars.

If you learn to find Andromeda, try challenging your friends to a contest. Ask them how far they can see at night. No matter what their answers are, you'll win.

Just point to Andromeda and say, "I can see for 13 million trillion miles!"

The Andromeda Galaxy

Since light takes time to travel from one place to another, we never see distant objects as they are right now. For example, light takes 8 minutes to get from the Sun to Earth. So, when you look at the Sun from Earth, you are seeing it as it was 8 minutes ago. When you look at Andromeda, you are seeing it as it was more than 2 million years ago.

Once, during a trip to Africa, I was shown a plaster cast of footprints that were a little more than 2 million years old. The footprints were made by ancestors of human beings called hominids. It was amazing to think those footprints were made more than a million years before the first humans looked at the sky.

That night, I saw Andromeda and thought, "The light I'm seeing right now set out from Andromeda at about the time the hominids left those footprints. Since then, humans evolved and gradually spread over our planet.

Great civilizations have come and gone.
But that light had so far to travel that
only now is it reaching Earth."

In our own galaxy, we can see clouds
of gas and dust where new stars are
forming. Other gassy clouds are the
leftovers of explosions where giant stars
have died. Humans were wrong when
they believed that the stars never changed.
The universe is constantly changing, but
so slowly that humans don't usually see
the stars change during their lifetime.

Our own Sun is about halfway
through its life as a star. About 5 billion
years from now, the Sun will start to cool
as it runs out of fuel. As it cools, its
gases will expand, until the Sun becomes
the type of star known as a red giant. It
will swell and swell until it swallows up
Earth. If humans are still around then,
they will have to find a new home in
space.

Of course, they have a lot of time to
figure things out. All of human history,

from the hominids to you and me, is just an eye blink in time compared to the long life of the Sun.

After rounding the Sun, Halley's starts to lose speed, like a roller coaster going uphill. You might notice that now its tail is in *front* of you. The solar wind blows out from the Sun, so a comet's tail always points away from the Sun, no matter which way the comet is traveling.

In a few weeks, Halley's will once again cross Earth's orbit on its way back out into space. After nearly 38 years riding the comet, you're going home.

Earth   *NASA*

Chapter Eleven

2061: Earth

Earth! All the places you have seen on your journey are beautiful in their own ways, but to human eyes none of them look as inviting as this one.

Somewhere among the billions of stars there may be other worlds where water runs and plants grow and animals play in the light of their sun. But for all we know today, there is only one such place in all the universe.

From out in space, you see right away what makes Earth special — it's wet! Three quarters of Earth's surface is covered with water. You haven't seen anything like this in all your travels through the Solar System.

Earth has water on its surface because its orbit is just the right distance from the Sun. A little closer to the Sun, and the water would boil off, as it has on Venus. A little farther away, and it would freeze into ice. Earth's orbit is just right for water, and for life.

Close by Earth, you see its large, gray moon. The Moon is too small for its gravity to hold an atmosphere, so it is airless and cold. Its huge craters were blasted into the Moon's surface by collisions with asteroids and other space rocks long ago. Earth has its own craters, but over time the flow of water and other changes in Earth's surface have worn away most of them.

The Moon is the only other world in space that humans
have ever visited.
NASA

Besides having water and air, Earth is special in another way. It is the only world in the Solar System that has been changed by living things. For example, plants in Earth's seas, where life began, soaked up some of the carbon dioxide in the early atmosphere and replaced it with oxygen. The new atmosphere made life possible for creatures like humans and animals that have to breathe oxygen to live.

We still depend on plants and trees to make oxygen today. Earth is a living planet.

Other living things — humans — are changing Earth, too. They are producing massive amounts of waste and pollution that are changing the makeup of Earth's soil, water, and air.

For example, many scientists worry that the gases from factories, cars, and other sources are creating a runaway greenhouse effect in Earth's atmosphere, like the one that happens naturally on Venus.

There is only one place in the Solar System where you
can see a scene like this one.

The result is global warming, a rise in Earth's temperature that could melt its icebergs, warm its oceans, and bring unpredictable changes to its weather.

These and other problems are waiting for you as you leave Halley's and return to Earth in the year 2061. Still, after your long years in space, you've never been so glad to call Earth home. You can't wait to feel grass between your toes, smell the sweet scent of pine trees, or taste a raindrop on your tongue. After seeing so many lifeless worlds, you could spend hours watching the miracle of a spider spinning a web or a robin feeding its young.

Meanwhile, Halley's is speeding away into space. Months from now, it will slowly lose its coma and tail. Away from the Sun's heat, its surface will freeze again under a new layer of black dust. Somewhere beyond Jupiter, Halley's will again become just a dirty chunk of ice.

And so it will remain, until more than 70 years have gone by and Halley's comes streaking back to the Sun. Then the story of the ugly duckling will repeat itself again, as it has for thousands of years.

With every trip around the Sun, Halley's leaves bits of its coma and tail strung out along its path through space. Earth's orbit takes it through this material every October, and people see a shower of "shooting stars," or meteors. Meteors are bits of dust, rock, and comet fluff that burn up in Earth's atmosphere. Meteors strike Earth's atmosphere every day, but meteor showers happen only when Earth passes through the litter left by a comet. Meteor showers are the ghosts of past comets.

Since Halley's sheds a little of itself with every trip, someday there won't be enough of its nucleus left to make a coma and tail. When that happens, Halley's Comet will never shine again. But that day is still many thousands of years in the future.

Halley's Comet streaks past Earth and its moon.

Halley's will be back again in 2134. What will Earth be like then? Will it still be blue and green and beautiful, or will it be choking in poisonous smog? Will its mountains still be capped with snow, or will global warming have melted the snow away? How many of Earth's precious forms of life will be extinct, never to appear anywhere in the universe again?

The answers matter, because we have only one Earth. It's true that planets are probably common in the universe. In just the past few years, astronomers have been excited to find more than 100 planets orbiting other stars. But no one can say how many planets are just the right size, and just the right distance from their sun, to have life — or whether life has started on any of them.

No one today knows how we could visit these distant worlds to find out.

It's only in the movies that starships zip around among the stars. The fastest spacecraft ever launched from Earth would take tens of thousands of years just to get to the nearest star.

Maybe one day, we humans will learn to conquer the awesome distances between the stars. In the meantime, we would do well to take care of our home planet. Earth is more than our birthplace. It is our spaceship, the place that keeps us, and all the living creatures we know, alive in the cold and dark that surround us.

As the old saying goes, there's no place like home.

A Space Voyage
Hitching a Ride Through the Solar System

Selected Sources

Angelo, J. A. Jr. *Encyclopedia of Space Exploration*. New York: Facts on File, 2000.

Arnett, B. "The Nine Planets: A Multimedia Tour of the Solar System." http://seds.lpl.arizona.edu/nineplanets/

Beatty, J. K., Petersen, C. C., and Chaikin, A. *The New Solar System*. Cambridge, MA: Sky Publishing, 1999.

Sagan, C., and Druyan, A. *Comet*. New York: Random House, 1985.

Seeds, M. A. *Foundations of Astronomy*, 6th ed. Pacific Grove, CA: Brooks/Cole, 2001.

Yeomans, D. K. *Comets: A Chronological History of Observation, Science, Myth, and Folklore*. New York: Wiley, 1991.

Selected Resources for Students and Teachers

There are thousands of Web sites devoted to space, many of which have wonderful pictures. Here are two places to get you started on exploring the Solar System through the Web.

"The Nine Planets: A Multimedia Tour of the Solar System, by Bill Arnett." http://seds.lpl.arizona.edu/nineplanets/nineplanets/

"Welcome to the Planets." National Aeronautics and Space Administration (NASA), Jet Propulsion Laboratory. http://pds.jpl.nasa.gov/planets/

~ Author ~

John Bergez

John Bergez has worked as an editor and writer since 1976. He has also taught professional editing classes since 1982. John and his wife, Jeanne Woodward, are partners in their business, Bergez & Woodward Book Development and Editorial Services. Much of John's editorial work is on educational materials used in elementary school, middle school, high school, and college.

In addition to writing several Start-to-Finish titles, John has written materials for school programs in social studies, astronomy, and other subjects. As a member of the school volunteer program in Pacifica, California, he uses Start-to-Finish books in working with fourth- and fifth-grade students on reading and writing. In recognition of his volunteer work, John received the San Mateo County Reading Association's Celebrate Literacy Award for 2001.

~ Narrator ~

Nick Sandys

Nick Sandys is a member of Actors' Equity Association and AFTRA and has performed in theaters in Chicago, New York, Dallas/Fort Worth, London, England, and Edinburgh, Scotland, as well as lending his voice to numerous

commercials. He is also a certified Fight Director with The Society of American Fight Directors and is the resident combat choreographer at The Lyric Opera of Chicago and at The Theater School at DePaul University. Nick holds an MA in English Literature from Cambridge University and is currently PhD(ABD) at Loyola University Chicago. He grew up in the ancient city of York, in the north of England.

A Note from the Start-to-Finish Editors

This book has been divided into approximately equal chapters so that the student can read a chapter and take a test or respond in writing after one reading session.

You will also notice that Start-to-Finish Books look different from other high-low readers and chapter books. The text layout of this book coordinates with the other media components (CD and audiocassette) of the Start-to-Finish series.

The text in the book matches, line for line and page for page, the text shown on the computer screen, enabling readers to follow along easily in the book. Each 2-page layout ends in a complete sentence so that the student can either practice the pages (repeat reading) or turn the page to continue with the story. Sometimes the last sentence at the bottom of the left hand page continues to the top of the right hand page. If the last sentence on the right hand page cannot fit on the page in its entirety, it has been shifted to the next page. For this reason, the sentence at the top of a page may not be indented, signaling that it is part of the paragraph from the preceding page.

Words are not hyphenated at the ends of lines. This sometimes creates extra space at the end of a line, but eliminates confusion for the struggling reader.